RAINBOW SHOPPING

QING ZHUANG

HOLIDAY HOUSE • NEW YORK

I feel as gray as a pigeon
on this rainy Saturday.
Not long ago, China was home.
But here in New York City, everything
is different, and everyone is busy.

Grandma is always nannying in a big house.

Mom pulls me out of bed like I'm a giant turnip.
She reminds me that today everyone
will be home for dinner! We need to go to
Chinatown to buy ingredients.

I jump up and get
ready to go.

The train ride is long, but Mom says it's worth it.

First, we head to the bakery.
Mom picks a sesame ball with luscious red bean
filling. I try the strawberry cheesecake.
We get a box to go. Now we shop!

I help Mom select the freshest garlic, ginger, and scallions.

Mom picks up a bamboo shoot. "This shoot can grow almost anywhere. Bamboo plants are flexible and strong, surviving the toughest storms.

Will you be my little bamboo?"

I nod, even though sometimes
I feel like crumbly soft tofu.

Up ahead are fruits from around the world,
piled up like jewels inside a treasure chest.

We go straight to my favorite:
persimmons—the redder the sweeter!

I marvel at the mysterious mushrooms.
Mom takes one that curls like thunderclouds.

"These will keep your hair healthy and black," she tells me.
"Black hair is so boring!" I say.
"Natural things are never boring," Mom replies, adding
it to the cart.

We walk through rows of vegetables in a hundred greens.

Mom bags the bumpiest squash.

"Not bitter melon!" I scrunch my face.

"Some bitter things are good for you." Mom smiles.

We explore long aisles of noodles, sauces, spices, pickles, and tea. We remember to get medicinal herbs for Grandma and numbingly hot peppers for Dad.

Soon we come to the seafood section, where the floor is always wet and the fish seem to stare.

When Mom goes up to the counter,
I peek around the corner . . .

It's the candy aisle!
I grab everything!

But Mom says I only get to keep one bag.

I think she must have eaten too many bitter melons in her life.

I help carry the groceries
to the subway station.

The subway lamps shine like
emeralds, guiding our way.

I hear the train coming, and my tummy rumbles along.

One more hour till home.

"You are pretty strong," Mom says. "I could not have carried all this without you, especially with my sore back!"

"You can pay me in snacks!" I say cheekily.

I feel my bags growing heavier and socks getting wetter. Mom leans her big umbrella closer to me.

When we get home, Dad and Grandma
are already inside!

We didn't get all the ingredients we
wanted, but Dad says it's okay.

"I promise everything will be delicious,"
he brags. "Watch and learn my kitchen kung fu!"

He slices the bitter melon paper-thin to make it less bitter for me.

He steams, boils, fries, and stir-fries.

Grandma and I try not to taste-test too much.

Everyone can't wait to eat!
Our dining area is warm
with food and chatter.

Mom and Dad bicker about
whether a dish is too salty
like always. Grandma
misses the seafood we
had in China, so hard to
find here.

A little different, but still yummy as promised.

Later on, I show Mom and Grandma my newest drawings.

Grandma tells me, "Your art reminds me of my mother. Life was rough back then, but I felt so loved wearing her embroidery. Her cut-papers brightened up our old home."

I try to imagine my great-grandmother,
a woman who lived in another time and in
a country that is now on the other side of
the earth from me.

"You must have gotten your creativity
from her," Mom says.

Everyone says good night as the rain
gets louder outside. I hear Dad snoring
immediately and Mom's slippers still
busying in the kitchen. Soon we
fall asleep.

In my dreams,
we walk together
in rainbow rain.